W9-BNE-357

A NOTE TO PARENTS

When your children are ready to "step into reading," giving them the right books is as crucial as giving them the right food to eat. **Step into Reading Books** present exciting stories and information reinforced with lively, colorful illustrations that make learning to read fun, satisfying, and worthwhile. They are priced so that acquiring an entire library of them is affordable. And they are beginning readers with a difference—they're written on five levels.

Early Step into Reading Books are designed for brand-new readers, with large type and only one or two lines of very simple text per page. **Step 1 Books** feature the same easy-to-read type as the Early Step into Reading Books, but with more words per page. **Step 2 Books** are both longer and slightly more difficult, while **Step 3 Books** introduce readers to paragraphs and fully developed plot lines. **Step 4 Books** offer exciting nonfiction for the increasingly independent reader.

The grade levels assigned to the five steps—preschool through kindergarten for the Early Books, preschool through grade 1 for Step 1, grades 1 through 3 for Step 2, grades 2 through 3 for Step 3, and grades 2 through 4 for Step 4—are intended only as guides. Some children move through all five steps very rapidly; others climb the steps over a period of several years. Either way, these books will help your child "step into reading" in style!

Copyright © 2001 by Berenstain Enterprises, Inc.
All rights reserved under International and Pan-American Copyright Conventions.
Published in the United States by Random House, Inc., New York, and simultaneously
in Canada by Random House of Canada Limited, Toronto.

www.randomhouse.com/kids
www.berenstainbears.com

Library of Congress Cataloging-in-Publication Data
Berenstain, Stan, 1923–
The Berenstain Bears and the missing watermelon money / The Berenstains.
  p. cm. — (Step into reading. Step 2 book)
SUMMARY: The Bear Detectives go to work when someone steals the money
Farmer Ben has made from selling his delicious and popular watermelons.
ISBN 0-679-89230-3 (trade) — ISBN 0-679-99230-8 (lib. bdg.)
[1. Bears—Fiction. 2. Watermelons—Fiction. 3. Mystery and detective stories.]
I. Berenstain, Jan, 1923– . II. Title. III. Series.
PZ7.B4483Behj 2001 [Fic]—dc21 98-54970

Printed in the United States of America May 2001 10 9 8 7 6 5 4 3 2

Step into Reading®

The Berenstain Bears
AND THE
MISSING WATERMELON MONEY

The Berenstains

A Step 2 Book

Random House 🏠 New York

Brother Bear here.

I'm a Bear Detective.

My partners are Sister Bear,

Cousin Fred, and Lizzy Bruin.

Our office is in a big hollow tree.

We share it with Dr. Wise Old Owl.

He's good at saying "WHOOO!"

He's also good at

"WHAT?",

"WHEN?",

and "WHERE?".

Sometimes he helps us on cases.

One day,

the detective business was slow.

Farmer Ben's

fruit and vegetable stand

was busy.

We went to help out.

Farmer Ben was known
for his fine fruit and vegetables.
But he was best known
for his watermelons.
Ben's watermelons were the
biggest, pinkest, and sweetest
in all Bear Country.

Everybody who was anybody
came to buy Ben's watermelons.

Grizzly Gramps came

in his pickup truck.

Chief Bruno came in his police car.

Mayor Honeypot came

in his long purple limousine.

Even Ralph Ripoff came.

He loved Ben's watermelons, too.

Ralph was a known crook.

I alerted my partners.

"Watermelons are too big to steal.

But keep an eye on Ralph

if he gets too close to

the apples, peaches, or pears."

We were very busy that day. Sister, Cousin Fred, Lizzy, and I packed the bags and carried them to the customers' cars.

Mrs. Ben took the money

and put it in the cash box.

Farmer Ben stood around looking proud.

We were tired and hungry
when lunchtime came.
We were glad to put up
the CLOSED FOR LUNCH sign.
We went into Ben's barn.

We had Mrs. Ben's tasty sandwiches
and big, pink, sweet slices
of Ben's watermelon.
Mrs. Ben wanted to keep the seeds
for next year's crop,
so we had fun spitting seeds
into a bucket.

Customers started arriving again
right after lunch.
We went back to work packing bags.
Mrs. Ben went back to work
taking the money
and putting it in the cash box.

That's when Mrs. Ben screamed,

"The money is gone!

We've been robbed!"

"Oh, dear! Oh, dear! Oh, dear!"

cried Farmer Ben.

Lucky for them we were on the job.

This was a case for the Bear Detectives.

Who could have stolen the money?

Not Farmer and Mrs. Ben.

It was their money.

The customers couldn't have stolen it.

There weren't any customers

during lunch.

Who could have done it?

It was a mystery:

the Mystery of the

Missing Watermelon Money!

We spread out and looked for clues.

But everything looked normal.

The cows were eating grass.

The rooster was watching over the hens.

The pigs were rolling in the mud.

The windmill was turning in the breeze.

The crows were stealing corn

under the nose of the scarecrow.

That's when Sister saw something
on the ground.
"Look!" she said. "Bits of straw."
"Those weren't here before,"
said Farmer Ben.

We followed the trail of straw
through the field.
"Hmm," said Fred,
"don't cows like straw?"
"Yes," I said.
"But cows have no use for money.
Cows didn't steal it."
Then Sister saw something else.

"Look!" she said. "Seeds."

"Those weren't here before,"
said Farmer Ben.
We followed the trail of
straw and seeds to the barnyard.

"Don't chickens eat seeds?"
said Fred.

"Yes," I said.

"But chickens have no use for money.
Besides, that isn't birdseed.
Those are watermelon seeds.
Chickens didn't steal it."

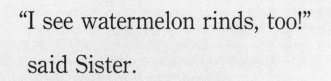
"I see watermelon rinds, too!"

said Sister.

"Don't pigs eat rinds?"

"Pigs have no use for money,"

I said.

"And pigs eat the whole watermelon,

rind and all.

They don't even spit out the seeds.

Pigs didn't steal it."

"Well, then," said Lizzy,

"who did steal it?"

It was a good question.

I tried hard

to come up with an answer.

"If I didn't know better,"

I said with a sigh,

"I'd say the scarecrow did it."

That's when I looked up and saw
Dr. Wise Old Owl taking a nap
on top of the
fruit and vegetable stand.
"Dr. Wise Old Owl!
Dr. Wise Old Owl!" I cried.
"Can you help us solve
the Mystery of the
Missing Watermelon Money?"

Dr. Wise Old Owl blinked and said:

"Note yon scarecrow—

he used to be thin.

You will solve the mystery

by looking within."

"Hmm, he used to be thin,"

repeated Fred.

"You will solve the mystery

by looking within."

We took a closer look
at the scarecrow.
Wasn't he looking a lot fatter
than he had before?
And look! A big pile
of watermelon seeds and rinds was
right at the scarecrow's feet!

Farmer Ben gave the scarecrow
a jab with his pitchfork.
"YOW-W-W!" cried the scarecrow.

Straw and rags
flew in every direction.
Who was "within"?

It was none other than Ralph Ripoff!
Bear Country's leading
crook and swindler was within.
And money was sticking
out of his pockets.

We marched Ralph back

to the fruit and vegetable stand.

Mrs. Ben called the police.
We could hear the siren
as the police car came.

Chief Bruno and
Officer Marguerite arrived.
"We caught him red-handed!"
said Farmer Ben.

"Considering the color of money,"
said Ralph with a guilty grin,
"I would say, 'green-handed'!"

"Cuff him, Officer Marguerite,"
said Chief Bruno.

Farmer Ben thanked us for our help.

Then he gave us the biggest, pinkest,

sweetest watermelon of all.

It was our reward

for solving the Mystery

of the Missing Watermelon Money!

We took the watermelon
back to our office and ate it.
It was the best!